Sweet dreams
to the young ladies
at the Academy of the Sacred Heart!

Lois

NIGHT SCHOOL

Written and illustrated
by Loris Lesynski

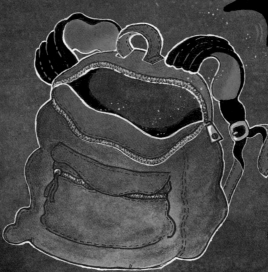

Annick Press

Toronto • New York • Vancouver

For Sam,
and other "night owl"
kids everywhere

© 2001 Loris Lesynski (text and illustrations)

Annick Press Ltd.

We acknowledge the support of the Canada Council for the Arts, the Ontario Arts Council, and the Government of Canada through the Book Publishing Industry Development Program (BPIDP) for our publishing activities.

Cataloging in Publication Data

Lesynski, Loris
       Night school

T 70371

ISBN 1-55037-585-7 (bound)
ISBN 1-55037-584-9 (pbk.)

I. Title.

PS8573.E79N53 2001   jC811'.54   C00-930200-X
PZ8.3.L54937Ni 2001

The art in this book was rendered in watercolor and colored pencil. The text was typeset in Utopia.

Distributed in Canada by:
Firefly Books Ltd.
3680 Victoria Park Avenue
Willowdale, ON
M2H 3K1

Published in the U.S.A. by
Annick Press (U.S.) Ltd.
Distributed in the U.S.A. by:
Firefly Books (U.S.) Inc.
P.O. Box 1338, Ellicott Station
Buffalo, NY 14205

Printed and bound in Canada by Friesens.

Interested in more of the night stuff
Loris found out about while writing this story?
Visit us at: www.annickpress.com

"I've told you ninety thousand times!"
his frazzled mother said.

But Eddie wasn't sleepy.
Just like every other night,
his brain was rock-and-rolling
and his eyes were nickel-bright.

Eddie was a night owl.
  He loved to stay up late.
"There has to be a place for me.
  Now wouldn't *that* be great!"

And sure enough,
  he found one,
on a list of special schools.
  "Sign me up," said Eddie,
  "for some better bedtime rules."

And so, one evening later,
  Eddie didn't go to bed,
but got aboard —
  at nine o'clock —
the Night School bus instead

He recognized a kid or two
   he knew from down the block.
They zoomed along the silent streets,
   then rumbled to a stop.

7

The Night School lights were blazing.
  The door was open wide.
Delighted and excited, Eddie
  rushed to get inside.

"A brand new batch of night owls,"
  said a teacher all in black.
Eddie shouted out, "Hello!"
  but no one nodded back.

It was just a *little* different from
  the school they'd had before.
The chalk was made of coal dust.
  There were sparkles on the floor.

The books had nighttime titles,
there were night lights
  on the wall,
and was *that* an
  all-night party
going on
  across the hall?

9

First of all, they studied owls,
   then lightbulbs,
      then the moon.

gas
bulb
filament
base

Some owls
shriek, but

They had such fun with werewolf howls
   that recess came too soon.

Recess was at midnight,
  but instead of playing ball,
  the children watched the late show
  on a TV in the hall.

URSA
MAJOR

Men

LEO
MINOR

Everybody Eddie knew
　　was probably in bed.
All his friends. His Mom and Dad.
　　He pictured in his head:
the teachers from his other school
　　in nighties fast asleep.
Imagine Gus who drove the bus
　　in pj's counting sheep.

"This is *great!*" said Eddie
　　to the children passing by.
　　"NIGHTTIME
　　　　IS THE
　　　RIGHT TIME,"
was the glassy-eyed reply.

There were
  lots of nighttime topics
for the stories
  they could write.

They studied just th

midnight zoo
moon visits
star wishes
night creatures
how bats live
all-night mysteries

Leopard

Raccoon

nimals that stay awake at night.

Eel

Tree Frog

Slow Loris

Opossum

About Bioluminescence

Many organisms exhibit bioluminescence, producing light. It is often found in...

Night Noises: bowl screech turn

Glow worms

Mouse

A+

Our Friend the Bat

Bats make ultrasonic sounds. Bats fly with great skill. There are over 950 kinds of bats.

Are Bats are furry mammals, not birds. The world's smallest mammal...

These little noises bounce back to their ears from any object they strike.

Bats like

Eddie was dismayed at lunch
to feel his eyelids closing.
He started on his sandwiches
to stop himself from dozing.

"A sandwich?" snickered someone.
"What a daytime thing to eat!
We get *our* snacks
from La La Max,
the nightclub down the street."

17

The playground was as dark as mud.
The air was cold and damp.

Each kid got a miner's hat, a flashlight or a lamp.

Back in class, they learned the nighttime spelling words by heart.

nocturnal

owl

moonlight

nightmare

midnight

party

There were only nighttime colors for the paints they had in Art.

Then

t h r e e a.m....

and

f o u r a.m....

a n d

t i c k ...

a n d

t i c k ...

... a n d

t o c k.

Eddie sighed. "This Night School has the planet's *s l o w e s t* clock."

21

His eyes were getting scratchy.
  His head was full of sand.
He felt too zonked
    to sit up straight,
    too conked to lift his hand.
What was that, so creepy,
    in the shadows on the wall?
  Eddie felt so sleepy he could
    hardly think at all.

"I wonder when it's *morning*,"
Eddie yawned behind his pack.
    "A new kid said
    the BAD word!"
shouted someone at the back.

New students — to the office!"
said the teacher with a glare.
The children wobbled to their feet,
and started up the stairs.

23

The second floor
    was even more
        peculiar than the first.
The third was cold and clammy,
    the next one smelled the worst.
    Was Eddie just imagining
    the ghosts along the halls?
    Were there monsters in
the corners, skulking low
against the walls?

The last floor
was so scary that
they didn't want
to stop —

25

— but the principal was looming
in a doorway at the top.

"You're just the kind of kids we want!"
  he said with fervent glee.
"I'm pleased to say your future looks
  as dark as it could be.
Now you'll go to school all night,
  and get to sleep all day.
Your dungeon rooms are ready.
  This is where you'll stay."

GRADUATING

NIGHTTIME
HIGH SCHOOLS:

-get
coffee for
students

NIGH

"But...but...but," said Eddie,
"but...but...what about our friends?
Our other school,
our homes, our rooms —
you mean this
never ends?"

Eddie started backing down
the dark and dusty hall.
"Night School is
a fright school,
not a proper school at all!
It's just a hoax
to make our folks
agree to let us come.
Let's *go!*" he cried.
The kids woke up —

—and broke into a run.

The creatures who were teachers
   cried, "We *have* to have you here!"
The race began. The children ran,
   their hearts a-thump with fear.

Grabbing! Snatching! Monsters close to catching them for good!
This was like a nightmare! Eddie led the best he could.

Then, suddenly: a brainwave!
Eddie wanted to rejoice.
He shouted out,

"*Good morning!*"

in his *most*
sunshiny voice.

The nighttime creatures halted,
ghastly faces all too near.
"Never, *ever*,"
came the whisper,
"do we use those words in here."

The grabbing stopped,
the snatching stopped,
they whimpered in retreat —

— and the children hurtled home along the early morning street.

Home at last…and Eddie found his parents at the door. "We missed you so! Oh, please don't go to Night School anymore."

Exhausted, Eddie nodded,
and exactly what he said
was: "MOMMY!
MOMMY!
DADDY!
DADDY!
LET ME GO
TO BED!!!
I beg you ninety
thousand times!
I could not
want it more!"

And sleep he did —
that day and night —
till life was like before.

31

So Eddie's back at day school,
  and he goes to bed at eight.
    Soon he'll find a better way
      to stay up really late.

He's glad he's not at Night School,
  but every now and then,
    he wonders what they're doing there
      — then goes to sleep again.